WILLOW'S WALKABOUT
A CHILDREN'S GUIDE TO BOSTON

Tail Print
This is what a
wallaby track looks like.

Written by Sheila S. Cunningham
Illustrated by Kathie Kelleher

Dedications

Sheila Cunningham: *For Kevan and Dempsey*
Kathie Kelleher: *For my two special guys, Ron and Luca*

Author Acknowledgment

First and foremost, I am forever grateful to my dear grandmother, Irene Dougher Donnelly, and beloved parents, John and Mary Lenahan, for instilling in me their love of language, introducing me to the joy of poetry, and sharing with me their wonderful wit. Additionally, I wish to thank my publishers, Ib and Carole Bellew, and my illustrator, Kathie Kelleher, for their respective expertise, for their dedication to this project, and for the kindness and friendship they have extended to me throughout our collaboration. Finally, I appreciate very much the guidance and technical support I received from my lovely niece, Virginia Lenahan, and treasured friend Philip Cutting.

www.bunkerhillpublishing.com
by Bunker Hill Publishing Inc.
285 River Road, Piermont
New Hampshire 03779, USA

10 9 8 7 6 5 4 3 2 1

Text Copyright ©2011 by Sheila Cunningham
Illustrations Copyright ©2011 by Kathie Kelleher
All rights reserved.

Library of Congress Control Number: 2012930409

ISBN 978-1-59373-096-3

Designed by Joe Lops
Printed in China by Jade Productions

WALLABY ESCAPED!

Special thanks are due to "Aardu," a most inquisitive and ingenious wallaby who, many years ago, went missing from the Stone Zoo in Stoneham, Massachusetts. This brave wallaby hopped unnoticed from the cozy comforts of a zoo home in order to experience a new adventure. Aardu's escape and voluntary return to the Stone Zoo made headline news not only in Boston, Massachusetts, but all across the United States.

Newspapers at that time followed this "wallaby tale," making the most of Aardu's great

MISSING: AARDU

Missing from the Stone Zoo in Stoneham, MA. If found, please contact the zoo immediately!

courage and determination to see what life was like beyond the zoo. Yet, remarkably, none of the press stories ever revealed the

details of Aardu's whereabouts while away from home. The readers who followed those news stories, adults and children alike, were left only to speculate about Aardu's travels as the details of Aardu's adventure remained a mystery.

That is, until now . . .

So, for all those who worried and pondered where Aardu wandered, come follow an equally determined Willow as she, like Aardu, sets forth on a delightful journey or "walkabout" through the wonderful city of Boston.

Little Willow loved living at Stoneham's Stone Zoo
All her friends were nearby. There was so much to do
Friends like leopards and bears and some monkeys, as well
Played all day with the wallabies—life was just swell

You see, Willow was a sweet young wallaby girl
With a pouch in the front and a tail with a curl
She had ears that were special—they made her stand out
For she used them to hear what the kids talked about

To best hear what her visitors might have to say
Willow turned her large ears a particular way
In her pouch she held both a small notebook and pen
To make note of the places they said they had been

Of them all, there was one place they spoke of a lot
"For vacation," they'd say, "Boston is the best spot!
It's a city with wonderful, fun sights to see!"
"Cool beans!" Willow thought. "Boston sounds awesome to me!"

Stone
ZOO
NEW ENGLAND

IN AFFILIATION WITH
FRANKLIN PARK ZOO
ONE FRANKLIN PARK ZOO ROAD
BOSTON

One time at the zoo she heard boys and girls say
"In mid-April in Boston it's Patriots' Day!
It's always on Monday and always great fun
It's the day of the city's great marathon run!"

So Willow prepared for her secret first trip
She computed the miles per hop, jump, and skip
She made lists in her book, watched the weather for spring
And she planned how to pack so she'd not leave a thing

BOSTON

TRIP PLANNER

TO DO:
- order tent
- clean out pouch

Signs of Spring
- sun higher
- birds

Directions
Head East!

She then ordered by mail a small foldable tent,
When it fit in her pouch, it was money well spent
Willow started collecting the things she would need
For her daring escape, when she'd go with great speed

When her items were packed and her plans made full sense
Late at night, in the fog, she sprang over a fence
And her pals, who were sleeping, were left unaware—
That her bed at the zoo was now suddenly bare!

Then she set off to Boston and Patriots' Day
Through the night, lights from Boston helped show her the way
As she sprang—boing! boing! boing!—she exclaimed with a smile
"This is just how I'll run every marathon mile!"

How to Pack

Pack
light!

good bye
friends!
I've gone on
a walkabout.
I'll be back.
Love,
Willow

Once in Boston, she searched for a spot for her tent
Then right on to the famed Public Garden she went
Near the pond in the Garden would be where she'd stay
On her Boston vacation and her nights while away

Willow noticed the Swan Boats were near as a hop
So she thought for her tour this must be her first stop
In a Swan Boat she sat, a young boy at her side
Just to Willow he said, "It's a wicked cool ride!"

To which Willow said, "Yes, and you're really so kind
To let me sit near you—you don't even mind!"
When she whispered that she was so glad to see him
He said, "Follow me to the Children's Museum!"

"That will be the next stop on my tour!" was her thought
And so Willow hopped to it—a ticket she bought
The exhibits—fantastic! She looked at them all
She was there a long time—she was having a ball

Then she jumped to the Harbor to get there so fast
As she knew the Aquarium would be a blast
Seals, sharks, penguins, and all types of fish from the sea
Made this Harbor attraction a cool place to be

The day ended with such a most glorious sight
From her cruise of the Harbor as sunset brought night
She hopped back to the Garden to pitch her small tent
She then ate, slept quite well, and of Boston she dreamt

Come the day, she took food from her pouch with her paw
In her notebook she checked off the places she saw
She looked over the list of fun sights in her book
To see many—the Freedom Trail must get a look

For these sights you must stay on a brick path of red
"You must look at the sidewalk!" the children had said
It helps tourists in Boston walk each twist and bend
Passing Faneuil Hall, and to Boston's North End

She was able to join a group tour on the Trail
Where she stayed to the back to make room for her tail
The Trail led to the State House with all its steep steps
Which she eagerly hopped up to watch the state reps

HERE LYES Y BODY
OF MARY
GOOSE

PAUL
REVERE

SAMUEL ADAMS

She jumped back on the Trail to the Old North Church site
With its famous high steeple and lanterns of light
Those old lanterns, as beacons, had warned Minutemen
"Of course," Willow thought, "there was no Internet then!"

On the Freedom Trail, Willow indeed felt so smart
She learned patriots fought to give Boston its start
She took in lots of history from sites all around
She even saw Paul Revere's House as she bound

At the end of the Trail, going through North End streets
Willow found the stores selling nuts, berries, and sweets
She took time to taste samples and buy her top picks
Which she stored in her pouch as her Freedom Trail mix

With the trail mix in paw, she continued to munch
She kept up on her tour, never stopping for lunch
Boston Garden arena she thought would be nice
To see Celtics' home court and the Bruins' home ice

All the sights on her tour brought her knowledge and fun
Then she added one more since her day was not done
She would finish the day with the city's must-see
The Museum of Science and Theater Omni

At the zoo she had heard lots of little ones tell
"It has dinosaurs! Bees! Chicks that hatch from a shell!"
"The Museum has IMAX—and musical stairs!"
"For stargazing? You bet—Planetarium's there!"

How exciting a day with the fun tours she took
By day's end, while at dinner, she opened her book
Willow looked at her zoo notes—her Boston sights list
For historical places that should not be missed

The next morning at dawn she sought more information
On how she could take public mass transportation
For the Kennedy Library she wished to see
She was told, "Oh, it's easy, you just take the T!"

T means "subway" in Boston—she rode it that day
To the library honoring late JFK
A significant site that looks over the sea
She had planned on an hour, but stayed almost three

On the T back to Boston she took a brief nap
And once back in the city, she paid for a map
Then she looked for the arrow that says, "You are here!"
And she thought, "Wow, what luck! Fenway Park is so near!"

COPLEY

FREE
IMPROPER
BOSTONIAN

Herald

The
Boston
Globe

For the home of the Red Sox is at this large park
Here the legends of baseball have all left their mark
In the city a Sox cap's on most every head
"We're World Series Champs!" lots of T-shirts have read

So she followed her map to the Kenmore Square site
Where she easily spotted the park for its height
Willow joined with the fans to head in for the game
In the park well known for its Green Monster wall fame

For it's over this green wall that home runs are hit
Which is why it's a popular place to go sit
Here the baseball fanatics all cheer on the team
And shout for the Sox not to run out of steam

What great fun, to mix in with the crowd at the game
All the fans sitting near got to know her by name
When the Sox got a hit, she bent into a crouch
And caught that home-run ball when she opened her pouch

CITGO

WILLOW!
WILLOW!
WILLOW!
GO WILLOW!
WILLOW!
YAY WILLOW!

17
8
11
12
24
3
21
14

1912
FENWAY PARK
100 YEARS

FENWAY PARK   AMERICAN LEAGUE   NATION
P   1 2 3 4 5 6 7 8 9 10 R H E P   INR P   INR P   INR P

At the end of the game as it turned a bit dark
All the hot dogs were eaten and fans left the park
It meant Willow had dinner and went on her way
To head back to her bed at the end of the day

It was off to her hideaway spot with her tent
This time bounding past beautiful stores as she went
Down through Boylston and Newbury Streets, hop, hop, hop
She was peeking in windows, not stopping to shop

The next morning brought sun and a breakfast of toast
And she thought of the things she would like to do most
"Well, tomorrow's the marathon, last thing to do
So for now I'll just hop, jump, and skip to the Pru!"

She heard *Pru* was the nickname kids gave to the mall
At the center of Boston—Prudential, it's called
There is something for everyone, that is for sure
And a spot where the tourists can book a Duck Tour

PRUDENTIAL CENTER

From the comments of visitors, Willow made note
That Duck Tours take place on an amphibious boat
The boat goes on water and land for its ride
Taking tourists through Boston, along with a guide

"Yippee!" Willow said as she was going aboard
She then joined with the children to "quack" as they toured
A Charles River ride was a part of it, too
She thought, "No one will believe this back at the zoo!"

Seeing Boston's great city while on the Duck Tour
Made this wallaby think she just had to see more
The Tea Party Museum she dashed off to see
Where they honor the colonists who tossed the tea

While there, Willow remembered there had been some talk
Of a view of the city from Boston's Skywalk
In her notebook she'd jotted the phrase "bird's-eye view"
And beside it had written "at the top of the Pru"

Back she hopped through the town to the Prudential mall
To this building that stands so incredibly tall
She looked in at its shops and cafés as she passed
To head up to its top with its walls made of glass

Then once Willow reached Skywalk Observatory
She looked out at the city and thought, "I can see
All of Boston and more from this spot in the sky
And can almost look down on the planes that fly by!"

At the top, a museum was just to her right
It's called Dreams of Freedom, and it's a great sight
There she learned, as she tagged along with a class trip,
How the immigrants came in to Boston by ship

The tour finished and Willow looked back at the view
Then looked at the clock and thought, "That's all I'll do!"
It was time for her dinner and then time for bed
To be rested for Patriots' Day just ahead

Dreams of Freedom

The next day she was set for the marathon run
She got up and out early to join in the fun
For the runners and Willow were all on their way
To reach Hopkinton, Mass., for the start of the day

On her way to the starting line Willow did hop
Off to Foxborough, Mass., where she made a quick stop
In the Patriot Place stores, the Pats Hall of Fame
And Gillette, home of the Pats' football games

Willow sprang on from there to line up at the start
Of the marathon race with all those who took part
She met athletes in wheelchairs positioned to race
To charge off to Boston at their very best pace

She joined runners who came just to give it a try
And she gave "two paws up" as they each passed her by
With crowds lining the roads to wave them on past,
Through the cheers they all traveled first to the last

On to Boston she sprang in and out of the pack
And in no time at all—Willow made her way back
With the finish line crossed, and the marathon run
She knew that her vacation was finally done

And she knew there were miles to hop before she'd sleep
Many miles of streets that were so long and so steep
Willow had to head home now—no reason to lag
For her pouch was now full with the baseball and swag

And though sad her adventure had come to an end
She was glad to head home to be back with her friends
So to Boston she turned to say "Bye!" with a wave
With her memories always to cherish and save

SKYLINE TRAIL

NORTON

MERRIMAC

BELMONT

STONE
ZOO

When she returned to Stoneham, she knew what to do
She jumped over the fence to get back to Stone Zoo
It was nighttime so she wasn't seen in the dark
As she tiptoed on past her zoo pals in the park

She sneaked into her zoo pen not making a peep
While her wallaby roommates were all fast asleep
She shared souvenirs with all her friends the next day
And told them what fun she'd had while she was away

And, while glad to be home, Willow began to think:
Did her notebook need paper, her pen some more ink?
And she started to plan her next fun "walkabout"
Her ears ready to hear where else kids talked about!